TEDDY BEAR, TEDDY BEAR

Retold by NICHOLAS IAN

Illustrated by MISA SABURI

Music Arranged and Produced by DREW TEMPERANTE

CANTATA
LEARNING

WWW.CANTATALEARNING.COM

CANTATA LEARNING

Published by Cantata Learning
1710 Roe Crest Drive
North Mankato, MN 56003
www.cantatalearning.com

A note to educators and librarians from the publisher: Cantata Learning has provided the following data to assist in book processing and suggested use of Cantata Learning product.

Publisher's Cataloging-in-Publication Data
Prepared by Librarian Consultant: Ann-Marie Begnaud
Library of Congress Control Number: 2015958212
    Teddy Bear, Teddy Bear
    Series: Sing-along Songs : Action
    Retold by Nicholas Ian
    Illustrated by Misa Saburi
    Summary: A classic song paired with colorful illustrations.
    ISBN: 978-1-63290-600-7 (library binding/CD)
    ISBN: 978-1-63290-653-3 (paperback/CD)
Suggested Dewey and Subject Headings:
    Dewey: E 398.8
    LCSH Subject Headings: Children's songs – Juvenile literature. | Nursery rhymes – Juvenile literature. | Children's songs – Songs and music – Texts. | Nursery rhymes – Songs and music – Texts. | Children's songs – Juvenile sound recordings. | Nursery rhymes – Juvenile sound recordings.
    Sears Subject Headings: Nursery rhymes. | Teddy bears – fiction. | School songbooks. | Children's songs. | Popular music.
    BISAC Subject Headings: JUVENILE FICTION / Nursery Rhymes. | JUVENILE FICTION / Stories in Verse. | JUVENILE FICTION / Concepts / Words.

Book design and art direction, Tim Palin Creative
Editorial direction, Flat Sole Studio
Music direction, Elizabeth Draper
Music arranged and produced by Drew Temperante

Printed in the United States of America in North Mankato, Minnesota.
072016   0335CGF16

ACCESS THE MUSIC!

SCAN CODE WITH MOBILE APP

CANTATALEARNING.COM

Do you have a teddy bear? Did you know that teddy bears are named after a president of the United States? It's true! Theodore Roosevelt was the 26th president, and people often called him "Teddy."

Turn the page to sing a song about teddy bears!

TEDDY
Roosevelt
1901 - 1909

Teddy bear, teddy bear, turn around.

Teddy bear, teddy bear, touch the ground.

Teddy bear, teddy bear, jump up high!
Teddy bear, teddy bear, reach for the sky.

Teddy bear, teddy bear, bend down low.

Teddy bear, teddy bear, touch your toes.

Teddy bear, teddy bear, turn out the light.
Teddy bear, teddy bear, say good night.

Teddy bear, teddy bear, turn around.
Teddy bear, teddy bear, touch the ground.

Teddy bear, teddy bear, jump up high!
Teddy bear, teddy bear, reach for the sky.

Teddy bear, teddy bear, bend down low.

Teddy bear, teddy bear, touch your toes.

Teddy bear, teddy bear, turn out the light.
Teddy bear, teddy bear, say good night.

Shh. Good night.

SONG LYRICS
Teddy Bear, Teddy Bear

Teddy bear, teddy bear, turn around.
Teddy bear, teddy bear, touch the ground.

Teddy bear, teddy bear, jump up high!
Teddy bear, teddy bear, reach for the sky.

Teddy bear, teddy bear, bend down low.
Teddy bear, teddy bear, touch your toes.

Teddy bear, teddy bear, turn out the light.
Teddy bear, teddy bear, say good night.

Teddy bear, teddy bear, turn around.
Teddy bear, teddy bear, touch the ground.

Teddy bear, teddy bear, jump up high!
Teddy bear, teddy bear, reach for the sky.

Teddy bear, teddy bear, bend down low.
Teddy bear, teddy bear, touch your toes.

Teddy bear, teddy bear, turn out the light.
Teddy bear, teddy bear, say good night.

Shh. Good night.

Teddy Bear, Teddy Bear

Hip Hop
Drew Temperante

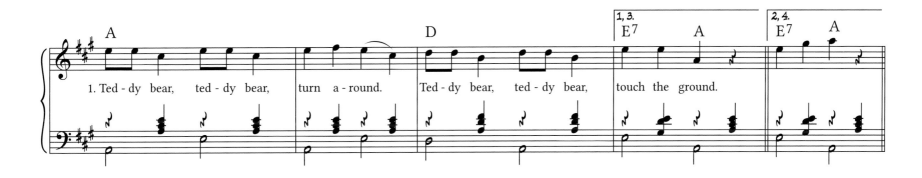

Verse 2
Teddy bear, teddy bear, jump up high!
Teddy bear, teddy bear, reach for the sky.

Verse 3
Teddy bear, teddy bear, bend down low.
Teddy bear, teddy bear, touch your toes.

Verse 4
Teddy bear, teddy bear, turn out the light.
Teddy bear, teddy bear, say good night.

Spoken:
Shh. Good night.

GUIDED READING ACTIVITIES

1. Do you have a teddy bear? What is its name? If you don't have one, do you have other stuffed animals? What are their names?

2. In this song, teddy bear gets ready for bed by turning off the lights. What are all the things that you do to get ready for bed?

3. Draw a picture of yourself playing with your teddy bear. If you don't have a teddy bear, draw yourself playing with one of your favorite toys.

TO LEARN MORE

Anderson, Steven. *Happy and You Know It*. North Mankato, MN: Cantata Learning, 2016.

Anderson, Steven. *Itsy Bitsy Spider*. North Mankato, MN: Cantata Learning, 2016.

Anderson, Steven. *Wheels on the Bus*. North Mankato, MN: Cantata Learning, 2016.

Borgert-Spaniol, Megan. *Head and Shoulders*. North Mankato, MN: Cantata Learning, 2016.